The Penguin
EDWARD KOREN

Cartoons by Edward Koren

Penguin Books

Dedicated to the memory of Bob Abel

Penguin Books Ltd, Harmondsworth,
Middlesex, England
Penguin Books, 625 Madison Avenue,
New York, New York 10022, U.S.A.
Penguin Books Australia Ltd, Ringwood,
Victoria, Australia
Penguin Books Canada Limited, 2801 John Street,
Markham, Ontario, Canada L3R 1B4
Penguin Books (N.Z.) Ltd, 182–190 Wairau Road,
Auckland 10, New Zealand

First published 1982

LIBRARY OF CONGRESS CATALOGING IN PUBLICATION DATA
Koren, Edward.
The Penguin Edward Koren.
1. American wit and humor, Pictorial.
I. Title.
NC1429.K62A4   1982   741.5'973   82-7492
ISBN 0 14 00.5334 4   AACR2

Printed in the United States of America by
R. R. Donnelley & Sons Company, Harrisonburg, Virginia

All but three of the drawings in this collection originally appeared in *The New Yorker* and were copyrighted © 1964, 1966, 1967, 1968, 1969, 1970, 1971, 1972, 1973, 1974, 1975, 1976, 1977, 1979, 1980 by The New Yorker Magazine, Inc. Three drawings in this collection originally appeared in *Harper's Magazine*. Many of the drawings in this collection also appeared in *Do You Want to Talk About It?* (New York: Pantheon Books, 1976).

"We deal with it by talking about it."

"April 20: The weather continues sunny and warm."

"Your work must be very satisfying."

"Our next speaker is a man depressingly familiar to everyone."

"I admire people like you, who can unwind with a hobby."

*"How were you born? Because your Daddy gave some of his
pollen to a bee, who gave it to Mommy."*

*"I love to hold your wing in mine, to touch your beak,
to ruffle your plumes . . ."*

"What would you say the precipitation probability is for today?"

"Broderick, what do you know about evolution?"

"Be gentle with it, men. It's a historic landmark."

"Anything you want at the store?"

KOREN

"Oh dear! It _isn't_ a boutique!"

"So let's have a big paw for a really great performer."

"It's a beautiful country, all right—if you can afford it."

"It looks like an (X) rating to me."

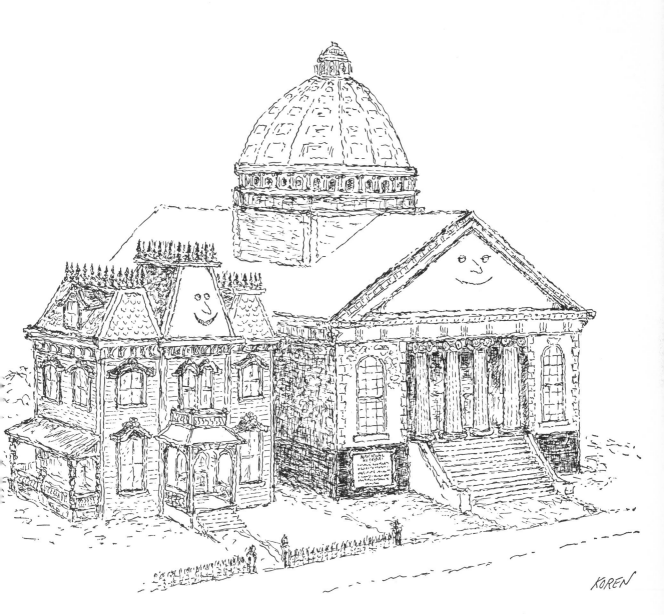

"What did they give you—National Landmark or Historical Monument?"

"One, two, three. One, two, three. One, two, three . . ."

"We've decided not to have children."

"There surely must be some mistake—I'm middle-class!"

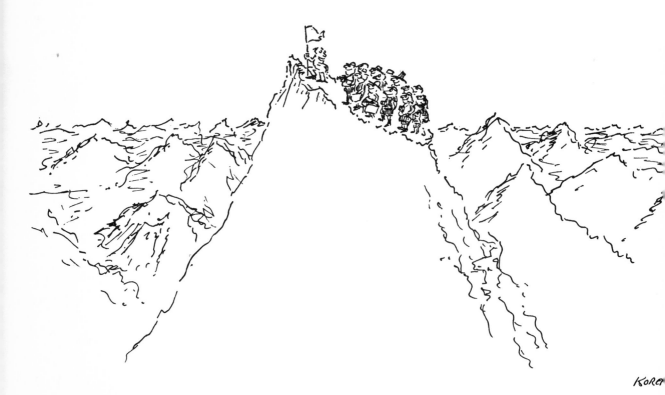

"This peak has never before been scaled by a group."

*"I used to be a management consultant, but now
I'm into making up songs and poems."*

"You grew up in the fifties, didn't you?"

"No more carbohydrates until you finish your protein."

KOREN

"*The sex isn't so much, but the violence is marvellous!*"

"Lights! Camera! Love!"

"It's such a thrill to meet the modern artist's modern artist."

"While I rather enjoy pistachio, almond fudge, and English-toffee twirl,
I think my very favorite is still plain vanilla with sprinkles."

"Tell me about your first wife."

"Ah, Hopkins! Finalmente!"

"What's it like to be at the top of the food chain?"

"Tonight we're not saying anything unless it's significant."

"They're much too permissive."

"Concept . . . generalization . . . articulation . . . conclusion!"

"I work four hours in the morning. Then meditation and errands."

"It fits you like a glove, sir."

KOREN

"You are an affront to the palate."

"You look disgustingly healthy."

"Do you have any identification?"

"Since we're splitting the bill, why don't you have something __really__ good?"

"I've got to install an anti-pollution device or get out of town."

"All power to the board of directors!"

"Talk, talk, talk!"

*"The question on everyone's mind these days is
'What is Middle America thinking?' Well, tonight we're going to find out."*

"Have you given any thought to what you'll do with your Saturdays when the world's fossil fuels are used up?"

"Happy?"

"I'm no stranger to the creative act myself."

"Yes, I __am__ into a new thing, dear child. It's called embroidery."

"Well, now we've seen it."

"Excuse me, but what's the nature of this bar?
Political, literary, or singles?"

"He's just been given the nod from the New York Zoological Society."

KOREN

*"Our next mind-shattering song is a simple A–B–A form which
relies on the rhythmic texture and variation of naive American marching
music and Renaissance madrigals."*

"Tell me, sir. Is it good or bad?"

"Extend your left rear paw behind you. Raise your right front paw
above your head and extend your left front paw straight in front of you.
On the count of four, breathe deeply . . ."

"Is it too cutesy?"

"Dickie, I hardly recognized you! You've changed your format."

"*I do think your problems are serious, Richard.*
They're just not very interesting."

"I am calling from an antique phone, Operator,
and I want Information, not Directory Assistance."

"Darling, let's get divorced."

"Air clean enough for you today?"

"William, do you have the courage to love?"

"And just what gives you the right to say that?"

"Would you scratch my back?"

"French, Italian, Russian, or Thousand Island?"

"Why such a long face?"

"Are you a hunter or a food gatherer?"

"*I'm sorry, but it just isn't working out between us, Jeffrey.
You're an orange, and I want an apple.*"

*"A brilliant achievement . . . Unflinching . . . Writing at its most
illuminating . . . Gripping . . . Explosive . . . Long overdue . . . True vision . . .
Plain speech . . . Proclaims the failure of our civilization as a whole."*

"I __am__ trying to share my feelings with you, damn it!"

*"What we'd like is a four-hundred-thousand-word novel
that oversteps the bounds of decency."*

*"We applaud excellence—regardless of the manner
in which it manifests itself."*

"Give me a for instance."

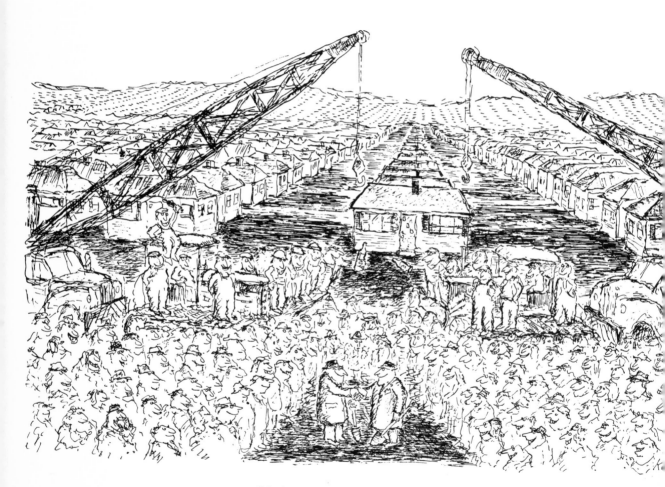

"At last! One nation, indivisible."

"*Young man, at table you either particularize
or generalize, but not both.*"

"One lyrical landscape—heavy on the Wyeth, light on the Expressionism."

"I'd like you to meet Frank Russ. He's just arrived on foot."

"Why can't you be more supportive?"

"He's one thousand years old today!"

"Wonderful seeing you!"

*"I just couldn't resist congratulating you boys.
Your music has contributed enormously to the vitality
of our culture."*

"With this sculpture, the current crisis between the object and the image reaches into the more fundamental conflict between the metaphysical angst of the first-generation Abstract Expressionists and the space-environment preoccupations of the avant-garde."

"He's charged with expressing contempt for data-processing."

"I know I'm being paranoid, but I think we should be a little careful about expressing ourselves too freely."

*"You're suffering from sensory overload.
Cut down on your intake of media."*

"You may be a sexist, but you're sweet."

"This is Captain Townley, ladies and gentlemen. Tonight we'll be flying in clear weather at twenty-nine thousand feet, and we'll be discussing the Role of Morality in the Technologies of Developing Nations."

"Yes, it is beautiful, but will it serve eight?"

"Loved the show!"

"Really, Susan! I never thought of you as the hysterical type."

"It's mighty good eating for the pennies it costs."

"They represent one hundred and nineteen years of experience."

KOREN